TEDD ARNOLD

HUGGLY AND THE TOY MONSTER

SCHOLASTIC INC. Cartwheel BOOKS®
New York Toronto London Auckland Sydney

To Camilla

Library of Congress Cataloging-in-Publication Data
Arnold, Tedd.
Huggly and the toy monster/by Tedd Arnold.
p. cm.—(The monster under the bed)
"Cartwheel books."
Summary: When Huggly the monster is accidentally mistaken for a toy and given as a birthday gift, it is up to his friends, Booter and Grubble, to rescue him.
ISBN 0-590-11761-0
[1. Monsters—Fiction. 2. Toys—Fiction. 3. Birthdays—Fiction.]
I. Title. II. Series.
PZ7.A7379Hr 1998
[E]—dc21
98-24834
CIP
AC

12 11 10 9 8 7 6 5 4 3 2 8 9/9 0/0 01 02 03

Printed in the U.S.A. 24
First printing, November 1998

"Look at what I found!" Huggly couldn't wait to show his friends, Booter and Grubble. He dragged something big and green into their Secret Slime Pit.

Grubble was folding a paper airplane. "What is that?" he asked.

"It's a toy monster," said Huggly, "and it looks like me! Watch. It eats stuff, it makes sounds, and it blows air like a dragon!"

Booter gasped. “It’s a people toy! The rule is: Never take people stuff. You should put it back before they find out it’s gone!”

“I took it out of its box,” Huggly explained, “and brought it under the bed so I could look at it without getting caught. Now I can’t get it back up by myself.”

“We’ll help!” said Booter and Grubble. “Let’s go!”

“Great!” said Huggly.

They hurried down several long tunnels to the steps under the bedroom where Huggly found the toy. "I'll go up," he said. "Then you two hand it to me."

Huggly peeked out from under the bed. “No people in sight,” he whispered. “I’m going up.”

He climbed into the room and found the empty toy box right where he had left it. “Okay,” he whispered. “Hand me the...” Before he could say any more, the bedroom door flew open!

Oops! thought Huggly. He had to get out of sight — and fast! Without thinking, he hid in the closest place he could find.

The people child hurried into the room carrying paper and ribbon. He wrapped up the box.

"Bernie's going to love this birthday present," he said, running out the door. "Time to PARTY!"

“What are we going to do?” asked Grubble.

“Follow me!” said Booter. They hurried back to the Secret Slime Pit.

It was dark inside the present. Huggly didn't know where he was. Some kind of party was going on and it was noisy. He tried to be still but his tail itched.

Then his head itched.

Someone yelled, “Time to unwrap the presents!”

Bernie saved the biggest present for last. When she unwrapped Huggly, she screamed, “It’s Ugzilla! Just what I wanted! Thank you, Wallace!” She lifted Huggly out of the box and set him on the table. He tried to act like a toy.

“The pizza is here!” someone shouted. Everyone cheered and grabbed a piece. Huggly didn’t know what pizza was, but it smelled good. He needed a snack. Maybe if he was fast enough, when everyone was busy eating...

He snatched a slice of pizza and swallowed it whole. The noisy crowd fell silent and looked at him.

Oops, Huggly thought to himself, *not fast enough*.

Bernie's eyes grew large. "Ugzilla," she said, "you have the deluxe, exclusive, gobble-swallow action jaws! You're the best toy ever!"

And she hugged him.

At that moment, back at the Secret Slime Pit, Booter was rummaging through her stuff. "Where is it?" she cried. "We can't find Huggly without it!"

"Where is what?" asked Grubble.

"My tunnel map," Booter answered. "We need it to get to Bernie's house and rescue Huggly."

"*Hm-m-m*," said Grubble. "Where did I see that map?"

While Booter and Grubble were busy searching the Secret Slime Pit, Huggly was still busy trying to act like a toy. Everyone at the party ate pizza as Bernie played with Ugzilla.

She moved his arms.

She pulled his tail.

She looked inside his mouth to see where the pizza had gone. Huggly let out a loud "Bu-u-u-r-r-r-r-r-r-p!" quite by accident.

Everyone stared at Huggly.

Oops, he thought. *Now they know I'm not a toy!*

Bernie's eyes grew huge! "Ugzilla," she said, "you have digital, superstereo, audiorama sound effects! You're the best toy ever!" And she hugged him.

Meanwhile, back at the Secret Slime Pit, Booter was still frantically searching for the tunnel map. "Think, Grubble, think!" she cried. "Have you seen it?"

"Well...," Grubble said slowly, "maybe it was under my bug collection."

"Okay," said Booter. "You look there. I'll check in my box of rocks. And hurry! Something terrible could be happening to Huggly!"

Terrible indeed! At the party, a big people person had put something on the table beside Huggly. And it was on fire! Huggly wanted to run away, but remembered he was a toy. Everyone started singing. No one seemed to care about the fire on the table. Maybe they wouldn't notice if...

Huggly blew out the flames.

The singing stopped abruptly. This time even the big people stared at Huggly.

Uh-oh! he thought. *Now I'm caught for sure!*

Bernie's eyes nearly popped out of her head.

"Ugzilla," she said, "you have the battery-powered, huff-and-puff, dragon-breath feature! You're the best toy ever!" And she hugged him again.

Just then, back at the Secret Slime Pit, Booter shouted, “Aha!” and she leaped at Grubble.

“Hey, that’s my paper airplane!” cried Grubble as Booter snatched it from his hands. “What are you doing?”

“No time to explain!” Booter said. “Follow me!” and she raced away.

Back at the party, Bernie said good-bye to Wallace and the rest of her guests.

After helping clean up the party mess, she carried all the new toys to her bedroom.

One at a time, she began putting her birthday presents into a huge toy chest.

Uh-oh, thought Huggly. *If she puts me in there, I'll never get out*.

Then he heard something behind him. *"Ps-s-s-s-s-t!"*
Huggly looked over his shoulder. Booter and Grubble were under Bernie's bed! Booter pushed the toy monster into the room and whispered, "Come on, Huggly. Hurry!"

Huggly dived under the bed just as Bernie turned around. She picked up Ugzilla, hugged him once more, and put him away.

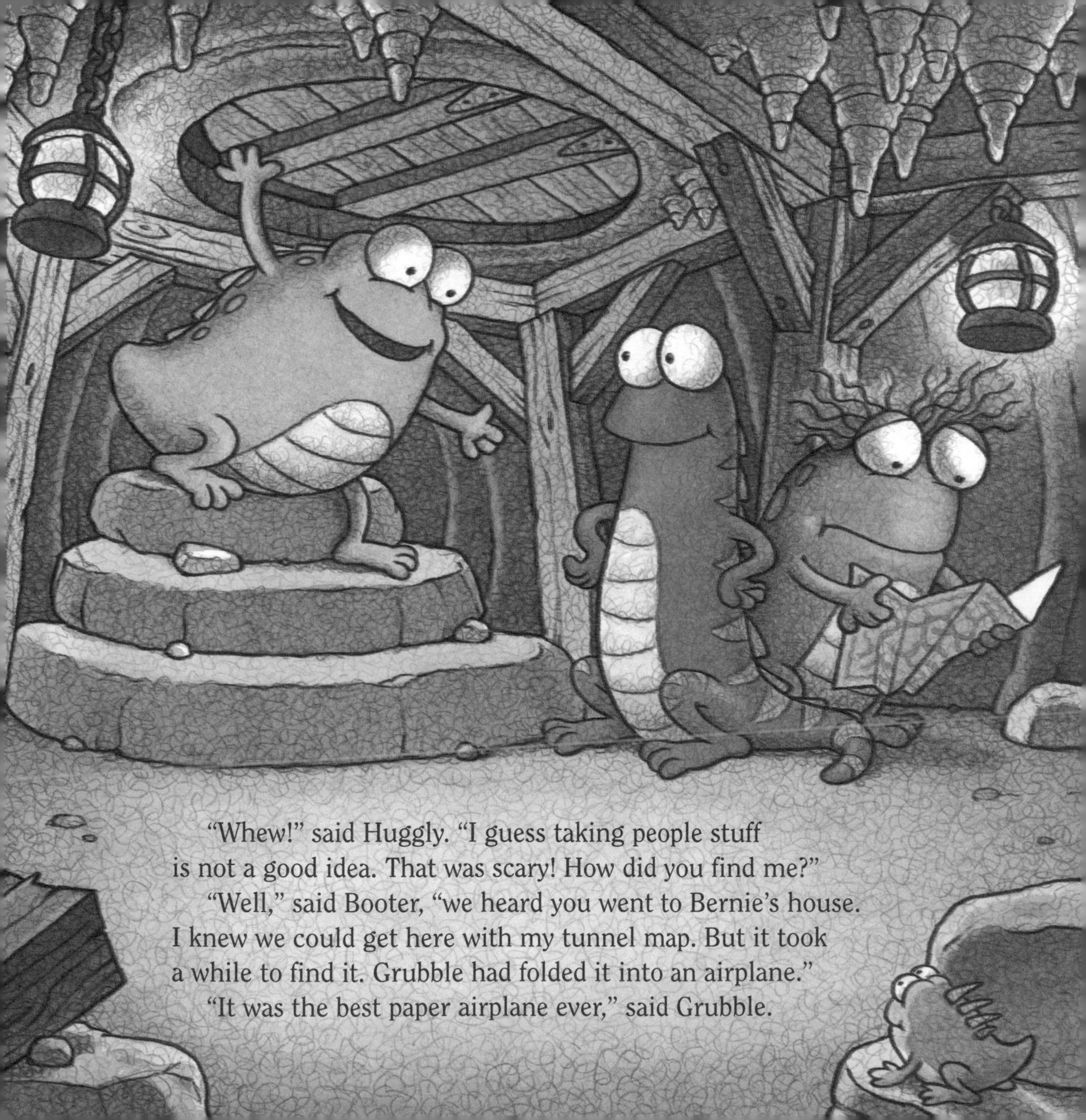

"Whew!" said Huggly. "I guess taking people stuff is not a good idea. That was scary! How did you find me?"

"Well," said Booter, "we heard you went to Bernie's house. I knew we could get here with my tunnel map. But it took a while to find it. Grubble had folded it into an airplane."

"It was the best paper airplane ever," said Grubble.

"Booter, Grubble, thanks for saving me," Huggly said. "You are the *best friends* ever!" And he hugged them.